TANA HOBAN

Is It Rough?
Is It Smooth?
Is It Shiny?

Greenwillow Books New York

This one is for Pierre Rouyer

Printed in Hong Kong
by South China Printing
Company (1988) Ltd.

First Edition

15 14 13 12 11 10 9

Library of Congress
Cataloging in Publication Data
Hoban, Tana.
Is it rough? Is it smooth? Is it shiny?
Summary:
Color photographs
without text introduce
objects of many
different textures,
such as pretzels,
foil, hay, mud,
kitten, and bubbles.
1. Surfaces (Technology)
—Pictorial works
—Juvenile literature.
[1. Textures
—Pictorial works]
I. Title.
TA418.7.H63   1984
779'.092'4   83-25460
ISBN 0-688-03823-9
ISBN 0-688-03824-7 (lib. bdg.)

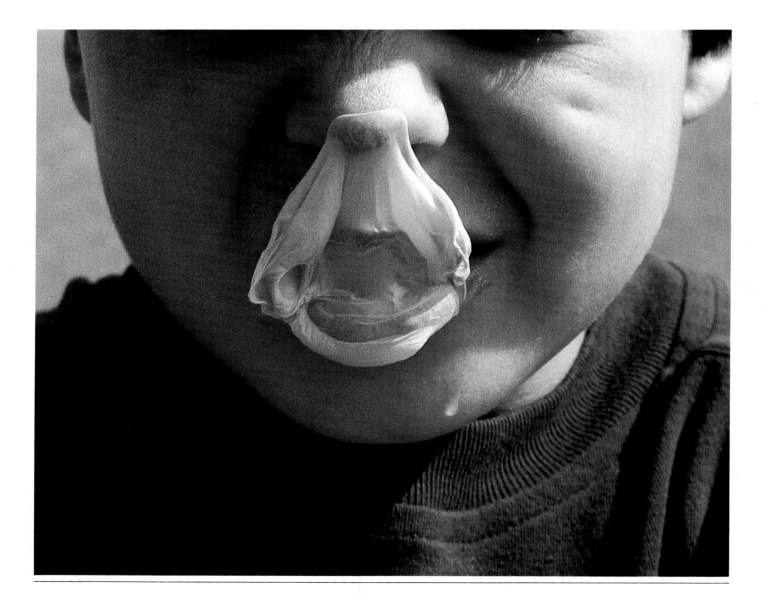

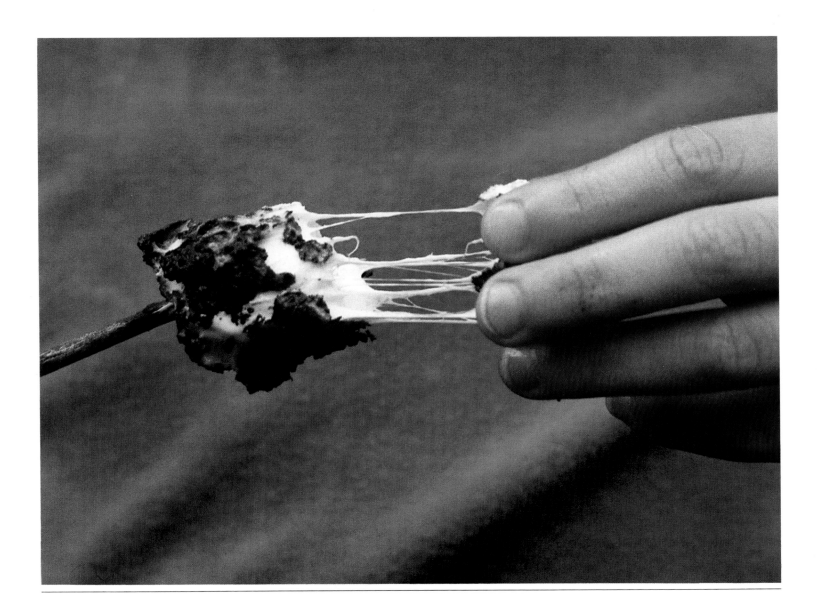

1 kg

DEMCO